Herman's
Letter

TOM PERCIVAL

Bloomsbury Publishing, London, New Delhi, New York and Sydney
First published in Great Britain in 2013 by Bloomsbury Publishing Plc
50 Bedford Square, London, WC1B 3DP

Text & illustrations copyright © Tom Percival 2013

The moral right of the author/illustrator has been asserted

A CIP catalogue record for this book is available from the British Library

ISBN 978 1 4088 3674 3 (HB)
ISBN 978 1 4088 3675 0 (PB)

Printed in China by C & C Offset Printing Co Ltd,
Shenzhen, Guangdong

1 3 5 7 9 10 8 6 4 2

www.bloomsbury.com

For Daisy and Leila

Herman's Letter

TOM PERCIVAL

BLOOMSBURY

LONDON   NEW DELHI   NEW YORK   SYDNEY

Herman and Henry had been best friends for as long as anyone could remember.

From tiddlywinks to climbing trees, they did everything together.

They had great fun inventing their own games and they even had a secret club with a secret code and a TOP SECRET handshake.

Everything was just perfect...

Until Henry had to move away.
The two friends were devastated but they promised
to write to each other and to stay best friends forever.

It wasn't easy for Henry to
settle into his new home.
He missed Herman terribly.

As soon as he could,
he wrote his first letter.

TOYS

CHINA

BOOKS

Herman Bear,
Herman's Hut,
The Wintery Woods,
Far Away.

HB6 4WW

Herman knew he should have felt happy for his friend but inside he just felt horribly, terribly, awfully...

JEALOUS!

It just wasn't fair!
Henry was off making new friends
while Herman was left on his own.

Herman Bear,
Herman's Hut,
The Wintery Woods,
Far Away.

HB6 4WW

UNITED STATES POSTAGE
2 CENTS

Herman Bear,
Herman's Hut,
The Wintery Woods,
Far Away.

HB6 4WW

Herman had **meant** to write back
but how could he possibly
tell Henry how miserable he was?

So hours, days and months
passed by and it was nearly
time for Herman to hibernate.

He settled down in his comfiest armchair, pulled up a blanket
and was just about to close his eyes when - WHUMPH!
- something clattered through the letterbox.
It was a letter! A letter from his best friend!

Herman Bear,
Herman's Hut,
The Wintery Woods,
Far Away.

HB6 4WW

Herman had never felt so happy. Henry missed him too!
He wrote a reply and rushed out through the snow to post it.

But he was too late.
The post office was shut for winter.
Herman groaned. What was he going to do?

Then he had a brilliant and rather bold idea.
He would deliver the letter himself!

Herman packed a suitcase and set out into the swirling snow.
He walked and walked and walked,
until his cosy home was just a distant memory.

He strolled past penguins,

tiptoed
through
caves,

and leapt over creaking crevices.

Then he climbed
and climbed
and climbed -
up steep cliffs
and frozen
waterfalls -
until finally...

SCRAAAAPE!!!!

SCREE EECH!!!

He reached the top of the tallest
mountain he had ever seen.

Poor Herman! His journey
had just gone from bad to worse.

Luckily, Herman was a very
resourceful bear.

But sometimes things don't go according to plan.

Herman bashed his head on a tree trunk and everything went...

BLAC

Herman's snoring attracted a lot of attention but nobody knew quite what to do.

Then somebody noticed Herman's letter.

It was obvious. What they needed was a postman!

Later that afternoon, Henry was very surprised to receive a strange, snoring box. He was even more surprised when he opened it!

Henry Raccoon,
The New House,
The Big City,
Far Away.

HR7 8BC

Henry read Herman's letter and chuckled.

He didn't mind Herman dropping in unannounced –
after all, they **were** best friends...

But he had forgotten just how **loud** Herman's snoring was.

Suddenly spring seemed like
a very, very long way away...

RRRRRRRING!!!!

But when it did come,
it was BRILLIANT!